Maggie de Vries

Illustrated by
Renné Benoit

TALE

of a

GREAT

WHITE

FISH

[a STURGEON story]

GREYSTONE BOOKS

Douglas & McIntyre Publishing Group

Vancouver/Toronto/Berkeley

EVEN BEFORE dinosaurs roamed the earth,
sturgeon swam in its waters. But though all the
dinosaurs died, the giant white sturgeon survived.
This is the story of one such great fish.

The huge fish spawns. She is old and her eggs
are many. Male sturgeon circle, releasing milt
over the eggs. Many are fertilized, many are not.

The fish spawns far up the mighty Fraser
River, above the canyon, where the bottom is
rocky and the water flows fast. Eggs gone, she
flips her tail, turns downstream, and begins
her long journey home to Sumas Lake.

The sticky black eggs rush downstream and
settle on the rocky bottom, one by one. Many are eaten
and others rot and die. But some of the eggs hatch.
After fourteen days, they have become larvae.

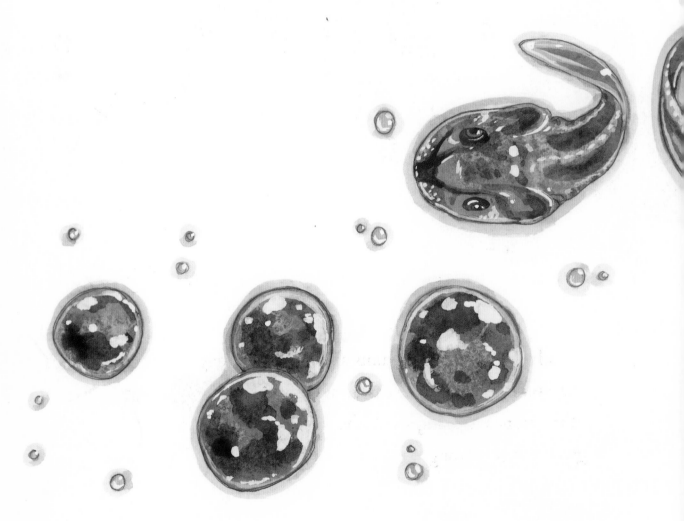

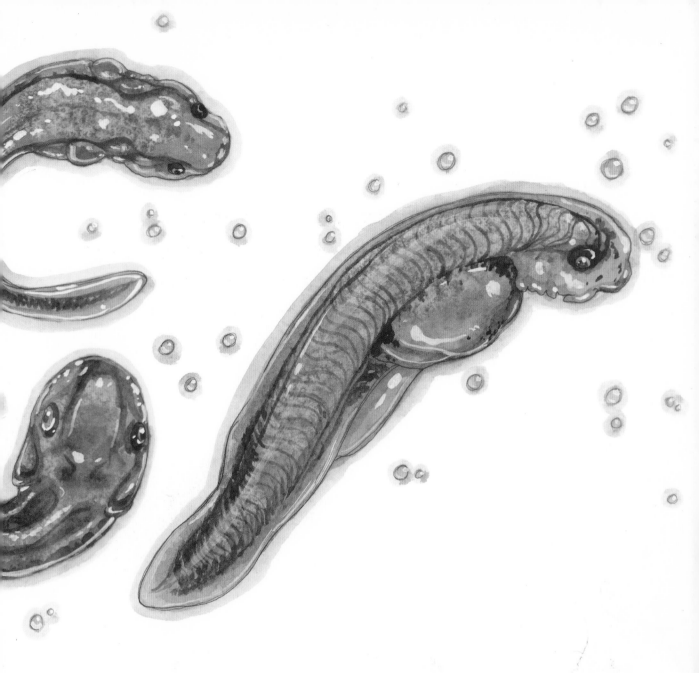

The larvae have little tails and big eyes. Along
the river bottom they swim, away from the protection
of the stones, seeking a side channel, a quiet place to
grow and get strong.

After a time, the larvae absorb their yolk sacs and become fry, the young of the year.

Among the fry is Little Fish, healthy and hungry. She swims and swims, eating thousands of tiny water creatures and their larvae. She knows she must stay out of the open. So she swims among rocks and sunken logs when she can. As the days pass, predators eat more and more of the tiny fry.

But Little Fish lives.

THIRTY YEARS LATER: 1858

30 years old

1.7 m (5.6 feet) long

32 kg (71 pounds)

Little Fish is no longer small. She is Fish now, ready to spawn for the first time.

Filled with thousands of eggs, Fish leaves the lake to swim up the Fraser, back to the place of her own beginning. Swimming upstream is hard, but her body tells her that she must.

Far up the river, the water runs fast and furious, but Fish is strong. She keeps going.

She swims past gold panners seeking riches. She swims beneath canoes carrying First Nations people from shore to shore. She swims through the clear blue water of the Thompson River as it mixes with the muddy Fraser. She swims back to the spot where she started out as a tiny egg settling among the rocks on the river floor.

After releasing her eggs, she turns as her mother before her and journeys back to the big flat lake.

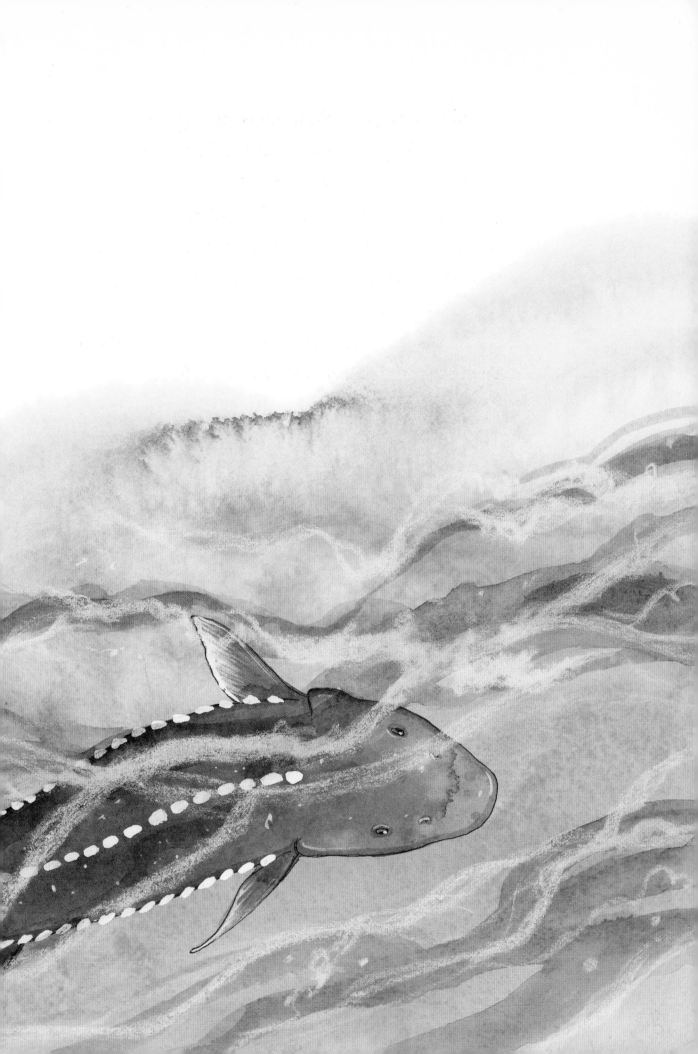

52 years old

2.7 m (8.8 feet) long

125 kg (276 pounds)

She is Big Fish now.

    Day after day she circles the lake searching for food. She drifts among the posts that hold the platforms where, away from the mosquitoes on the shore, the people of the lake rest. They catch smaller fish, but they honor Big Fish and others like her, for these fish are old. To the Stó:lō people, these fish are sacred.

69 years old

3.3 m (10.9 feet) long

263 kg (580 pounds)

Spring arrives, and Big Fish is hungry. One evening, she smells eulachon on the incoming tide and heads downstream. There, thousands of hooks fill the river, shore to shore.

Big Fish follows the smell, finds a small fish, and mouths it gently. But when she sucks it in, a hook pierces her mouth and she is caught. The more she struggles, the deeper the hook digs.

Fishers come to haul in their catch. They shout with excitement when they find Big Fish on their line, but she fights harder when she feels the pull from above. Finally, Big Fish is still, and they tow her close to shore.

Two men jump into the water and tie a thick rope around her body, behind her fins. The horse's hooves dig into the mud as the animal struggles to pull Big Fish ashore. The men untie the rope before they move on to claim the next fish. They will return.

Big Fish lies on the mud as if she were dead.

"The biggest yet!" a voice shouts.

Four boys, barefoot and in tattered clothes, stand over Big Fish.

"Are the men really gone?" whispers a more cautious voice.

"Aye, for the moment," says a third. "We'll take huge slabs. My mum will be so happy tonight!"

The loud voice speaks again now. "No. We'll do no cutting. This fish is big, and that means old." He crouches low. "I'll tell you something else. This fish is alive."

They do not believe him, but each boy there has lost to him when words came to fists. With a grunted "huh" and a "huh" and a "huh," they push Big Fish down the slippery bank and back into the river.

The boys stand on the bank. Big Fish
floats in the shallows.

"It's alive, I tell you," says that loud voice,
not so loud now.

"It's not. I'm going in after it. My mum's
counting on me for our supper."

Big Fish twitches then, and the children
shout, some with joy, others with regret.

But they all send up a cheer when her tail
flips, and she is away, back to the big flat lake
where hooks do not hide beneath the water
from shore to shore.

85 years old

3.8 m (12.5 feet) long

364 kg (802 pounds)

Big Fish has spawned five times in her long life. Each time, she has swum north through the great canyon. Each time, she has released more eggs than the time before.

The way is always hard. This time, though, the riverbed shakes as she reaches the narrow canyon. The water tumbles. Big Fish struggles to swim on.

Other fish, alive and dead, fly past. The river fills with noise. Rocks block her path. For hours, she noses forward, seeking a way through.

At last, Big Fish turns back and begins to search for a new place to spawn.

96 years old

4.1 m (13.4 feet) long

418 kg (922 pounds)

The platforms on stilts, the peaceful, floating boats—all are gone. Slowly, so slowly that a fish cannot know, the lake is draining away.

This time, Big Fish is almost too late when she begins her journey to the river. She slithers along the lake bottom, feeling her way through the muddy water.

When she finally reaches the river, she must swim through a maze of gill nets. At last, Big Fish finds a quiet spot under the docks of the great city of New Westminster.

More than once, she tries to return to the big flat lake, but it is no longer there.

FORTY-FOUR YEARS LATER: LATE SPRING, 1968

140 years old

5.2 m (17 feet) long

616 kg (1,358 pounds)

When she was younger, Big Fish sometimes jumped
high out of the water. She does not jump often now.
Then, early one morning, she does.

Eyes wide, a boy watches from a nearby dock. That
boy will remember Big Fish for the rest of his life.

TWENTY-FIVE YEARS LATER: 1993

165 years old

5.8 m (19 feet) long

722 kg (1,592 pounds)

Sturgeon are washing up dead on the shores
of the Fraser, their bellies filled with salmon.
No one knows why they are dying. People
are worried about the sturgeon.

 Fewer fish swim in the river now.

 Still, Big Fish lives.

 Sport fishers go after the sturgeon. Three
times Big Fish is hooked, and three times
she fights free.

TWELVE YEARS LATER: 2005

177 years old

6.1 m (20 feet) long

770 kg (1,698 pounds)

One day, Big Fish is hooked again, but this time she cannot free herself.

The fishers tow her to shore, and a man and a woman jump into the water. But they do not tie a rope around Big Fish. These fishers are studying the sturgeon in the Fraser River. They are trying to help them survive. They measure Big Fish and inject a tiny glass capsule behind the hard plate in her head. It carries a code that identifies her. The man and the woman release Big Fish back into the river.

"There she goes," says the captain. He smiles as he remembers the jumping fish he saw so long ago.

For years now, Big Fish has been hungry much of the time. Food is scarce, and she faces constant threats.

But she will not face death at the hands of fishers. Laws now protect her. And men and women will continue to study her. Each time they catch her, they will scan the glass capsule and know how far she has traveled and how much she has grown.

Slowly, they are learning the needs of the great white sturgeon. Perhaps now more of Big Fish's thousands of offspring will live from one century into the next and the one after that.

Sturgeon Facts

> Sturgeon have no teeth. They eat by sticking out their rubbery, tube-like mouths and sucking up food like vacuum cleaners.

> If a sturgeon gets enough to eat, it will keep growing its whole life. Very old sturgeon can be more than 6 m (20 feet) long.

> Caviar, the salted roe (eggs) of some species of sturgeon, is one of the most expensive foods in the world.

> The lower Fraser River was once filled with white sturgeon. Then in the late 1800s and early 1900s, many thousands of sturgeon were killed for their meat and roe.

> Many human activities threaten the sturgeon and their habitats. These activities include fishing with nets, building dams and dikes, polluting the river, and removing sand and gravel from river bottoms.

> In 1913, the Hells Gate Slide changed the water flow in the Fraser River and made it very difficult for white sturgeon and other migrating fish to pass through. The rock slide was caused by shaking from the construction of a railway.

> In 1924, Sumas Lake was drained to create more farmland in the Fraser Valley. This lake had been the home of many sturgeon.

> Provincial and federal laws now protect Canada's white sturgeon. All sturgeon caught (by nets or angling) must be released unharmed.

White Sturgeon

(SPECIES: *Acipenser transmontanus*)

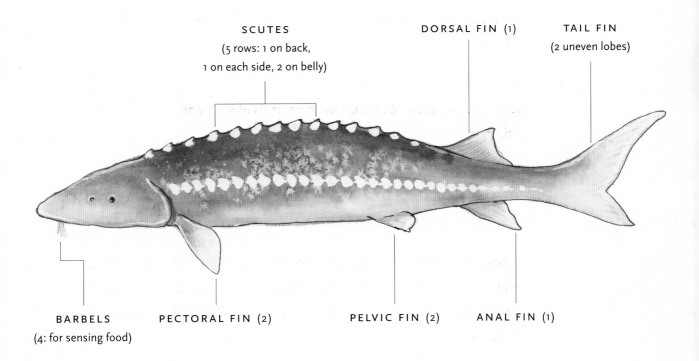

SCUTES
(5 rows: 1 on back,
1 on each side, 2 on belly)

DORSAL FIN (1)

TAIL FIN
(2 uneven lobes)

BARBELS
(4: for sensing food)

PECTORAL FIN (2)

PELVIC FIN (2)

ANAL FIN (1)

Glossary

EULACHON A type of smelt that dies after spawning. Eulachon are an important food source for Fraser River white sturgeon.

FERTILIZE To make an egg able to develop into a new life. Male fish do this by releasing milt over the eggs that a female releases.

FRY The stage of life a larva enters after it has absorbed its yolk sac.

GILL NET A long net that hangs in the water and is held in place by floats on top and weights along the bottom. Hundreds of fish can be caught in a single net.

GOLD PANNERS People who search for gold in waterways, using a shallow sieve or pan.

LARVA (plural, larvae) The stage of a fish's life after the egg hatches. The larva still has its yolk sac attached.

MILT The substance that male fish release to fertilize eggs.

SCUTES Rows of bony plates on a sturgeon's back, sides, and belly.

SPAWN To release eggs or milt. A female white sturgeon can release several hundred thousand eggs at one time.

YOLK SAC A yolk-filled pouch attached to a larva when it hatches from the egg. The larva absorbs the nutrients in the yolk sac to live and grow. When the yolk sac is gone, the larval stage is over, and the tiny sturgeon is called a fry.

Letter *from* Rick Hansen

Dear Readers,

Some of my most memorable adventures as a boy were exploring and fishing on the Fraser River.

I especially remember looking out across the river one day and seeing an enormous fish shake itself free of the water in a powerful jump, then fall back in with a huge splash. This incredible sight remains with me to this day—perhaps because of the almost impossible size of that fish, or maybe because of its ancient appearance.

When my friends and I learned that these white sturgeon were endangered, we became concerned about their future and their environment. To help protect these precious fish and their aquatic ecosystem, we formed the Fraser River Sturgeon Conservation Society. Many volunteers from government, First Nations, recreational and commercial fishing, and other groups began to work together to tell more people about these endangered fish and to help protect white sturgeon for future generations.

I hope this story inspires you to discover more about white sturgeon and to tell people about what you learn. We can all make a difference in the future of these wonderful creatures and their habitat.

Sincerely,

RICK HANSEN, C.C., O.B.C.

Rick Hansen was the little boy on the riverbank. Today, he volunteers as chairman of the Fraser River Sturgeon Conservation Society (www.frasersturgeon.com). He is better known as the first person to go around the world in a wheelchair, to raise funds for and help support people with spinal cord injuries. He is President of the Rick Hansen Man in Motion Foundation (www.rickhansen.com), which continues that work.

To Wendy Sutton, who brought this book to me. —MdeV
For Dave. —RB

Text copyright © 2006 by Rick Hansen Foundation
Illustrations copyright © 2006 Renné Benoit
First paperback edition published in 2007

07 08 09 10 11   5 4 3 2 1

Greystone Books
A division of Douglas & McIntyre Ltd.
2323 Quebec Street, Suite 201
Vancouver, British Columbia
Canada V5T 4S7
www.greystonebooks.com

Library and Archives Canada Cataloguing in Publication
De Vries, Maggie
Tale of a great white fish : a sturgeon story /
Maggie de Vries ; illustrated by Renné Benoit.

ISBN-10: 1-55365-125-1 (bound) · ISBN-13: 978-1-55365-125-3 (bound)
ISBN-10: 1-55365-303-3 (paper) · ISBN-13: 978-1-55365-303-5 (paper)

1. White sturgeon—British Columbia—Fraser River—Juvenile literature.
2. White sturgeon—Habitat—British Columbia—Fraser River—
Juvenile literature. I. Benoit, Renné II. Title.
QL638.A25D49 2006   j597'.42   C2005-905977-X

Editing by Kathy Vanderlinden
Cover and text design by Peter Cocking
Cover illustrations by Renné Benoit
Printed and bound in China by C&C Offset Printing Co., Ltd.
Printed on acid-free paper
Distributed in the U.S. by Publishers Group West

We gratefully acknowledge the financial support of the Canada Council
for the Arts, the British Columbia Arts Council, and the Government of
Canada through the Book Publishing Industry Development Program
(BPIDP) for our publishing activities.

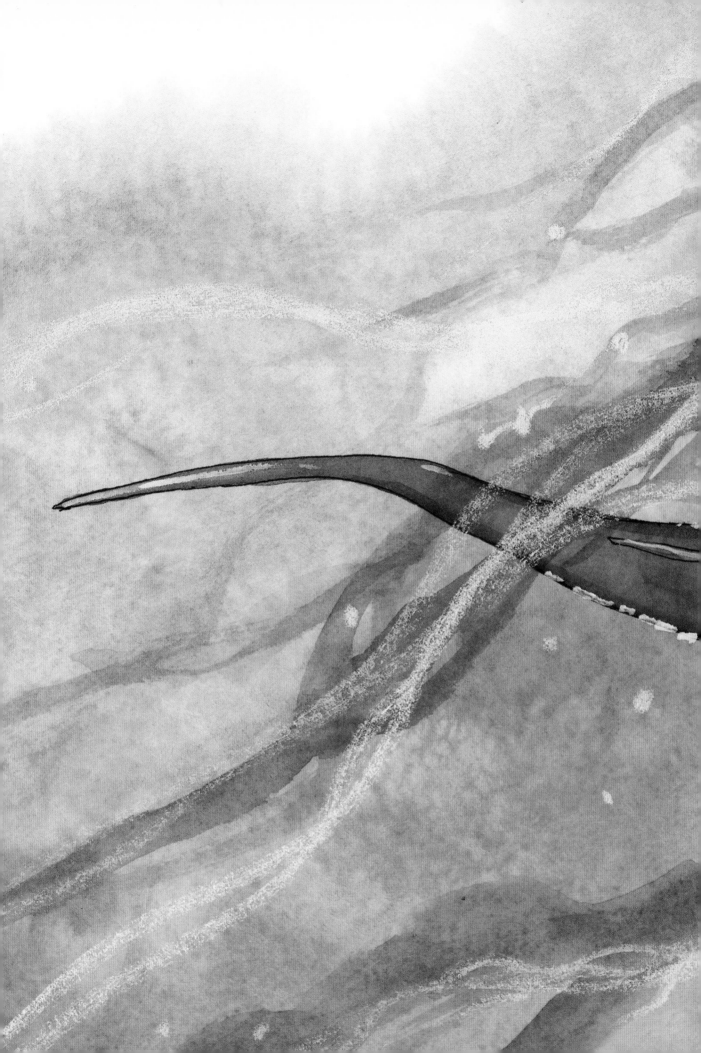